I0537850

WHEN LOVE BREAKS THE SILENCE

WHEN LOVE BREAKS THE SILENCE

NURISS CLARK

ISBN: 978-1-969913-98-3

For permissions or inquiries, contact:
Nuriss Clark
Email: Nurisslife@gmail.com

DEDICATION

To God, who in the quietest silence still whispers with love, and who turns every tear into a seed of hope. Without Him, not a single word of this story would have come to life. This novel is, above all, a testimony that His love holds everything together—even when the world seems to fall apart.

To all who have carried the weight of whispers, criticism, or rejection. To those who once believed their voice was not enough, that their story was not worth telling, or that true love was only a distant dream. This book is for you—a reminder that what God joins together, no one can tear apart, and that there will always be a power greater than any silence that tries to drown you out.

And to the hearts that still believe in tenderness, in faith that lifts, in hope that restores, and in love that transforms.

May these pages be a shelter, an embrace, and a promise that there is always, always a way when the heart holds fast to what is eternal.

INTRODUCTION

There are loves that are born in silence—like a timid whisper that barely dares to breathe. There are loves that grow in the midst of murmurs, among judging eyes and condemning voices. And there are loves that, despite everything, rise stronger than walls, firmer than prejudice, truer than appearances.

This is the story of Esther and Ron. She—a simple young woman from a humble neighborhood, with quiet dreams and a heart full of faith. He—the son of a respected family, with a future mapped out by the will of others and the weight of a name. Two paths that, it seemed, should never have crossed... yet within God's house they found a meeting place no silence could extinguish.

What you are about to read is not merely a Christian romance novel. It is a reflection of what happens when faith holds the heart steady in the storm, when love dares to defy opposition, and when the soul clings to the promise that nothing—not even the cruelest rumors—can silence what God has joined together.

Here begins a journey of deep emotions, of tears and smiles, of trials that seem insurmountable and of a hope that never dies. For in the end, there will always be a voice that rises above fear, above rejection, above the darkness...

A voice that breaks the silence.

TABLE OF CONTENTS

Prologue. 13
A voice of faith and hope anticipates the story of Esther and Ron.

Chapter 1: A Bench in the Park 15
Esther's earliest memories, her humble life, and her first
encounters with Ron in the congregation.

Chapter 2: Whispers in the Shadows 21
The awakening of secret love, their first meetings, and the risk
of being discovered.

Chapter 3: Silent Promises. 27
The neighborhood begins to whisper, and Esther struggles
against shame and fear.

Chapter 4: The Shadow in the Park 33
Ron and Esther cling to each other, knowing their secret can no
longer be contained.

Chapter 5: A Voice in the Shadows 39
Tenderness reaches its highest point as they share their first
sincere expression of love.

Chapter 6: A Refuge for Two 43
Sweet, intimate moments where they feel safe from the world
around them.

Chapter 7: The Weight of Whispers 47
The neighborhood turns cruel, Rosa fuels gossip,
and Esther feels exposed.

Chapter 8: Faith in the Midst of Despair 51
The rumors intensify, tension rises, and Esther begins to break.

Chapter 9: The Storm Breaks 57
Emilio catches Ron and Esther together in the plaza,
humiliating them before everyone.

Chapter 10: Esther's Breaking Point 63
Esther collapses and finds refuge in faith; Ron grows desperate
and seeks a way forward. Aunt Lorena steps in.

Chapter 11: Public Humiliation at Church 71
Emilio forbids Esther from participating in the congregation,
publicly shaming her once again.

Chapter 12: Secrets and Hidden Hope 77
Through Mateo, Ron manages to reach Esther with a letter full
of love and hope.

Chapter 13: The Storm Breaks. 83
With the strength of their faith and love, they confront Emilio
one last time and finally walk together without fear.

Epilogue 97
The humble wedding of Esther and Ron, celebrated with
tenderness and hope, marked by Emilio's symbolic gesture
of reconciliation.

Acknowledgments 105

PROLOGUE

Some stories are whispered into the world, too fragile at first to be spoken aloud. They are born in hidden places—between glances, between prayers, between the quiet beating of two hearts that dare to dream.

This is one of those stories.

It begins with silence.

The silence of judgmental eyes.

The silence of voices that wound without speaking.

The silence of a world that says, *You do not belong together.*

But love has never bowed to silence. Love listens to a greater voice—the voice of God, who unites what no one else can separate, who writes stories no rumor can erase, who gives courage when everything else tries to suffocate hope.

Esther never imagined that her quiet, ordinary life would lead her to such love. Ron never thought he would have to choose between the will of his family and the will of his own heart. Yet in the house of God, where whispers turn into prayers, their paths crossed. And once they did, nothing could keep them apart—not rejection, not opposition, not even the heaviest silence.

What you are holding in your hands is not just a Christian romance novel. It is a journey of faith and love, of trials and victories, of tears that become prayers and prayers that become miracles.

As you turn these pages, prepare to laugh, to cry, to feel your heart ache and then soar with hope. For this is more than a story of two people—it is a testimony that when love breaks the silence, heaven itself rejoices.

And once you begin, you will not want to stop until you discover how far love, faith, and hope can carry a soul that refuses to surrender.

Because love—true love—was never meant to stay silent.

CHAPTER 1

A BENCH IN THE PARK

I've never had much. I've known that for as long as I can remember. At home we never had extra, but we also never lacked the essentials: a tin roof that beat like a drum when it rained, a small room I shared with my younger sister, and my mother's hardworking hands. She would come home exhausted from cleaning houses all day, her back bent, but she never once failed to greet me with a smile.

I grew up clutching coins tightly before getting on the bus, saving my only nice blouse for Sundays, and asking nothing of anyone but God.

Maybe that's why I learned to walk lightly. My purse was always small—just enough to hold a worn New Testament, a mirror I'd inherited from my grandmother, and a pink plastic comb. I didn't carry more because I didn't have more, and honestly, I didn't need it. Simplicity had taught me to be grateful for the smallest things.

Sundays were always special. Since I was a child, my mother would take us by the hand to the neighborhood church, with its plain façade and wooden pews that creaked with every movement. There I grew up singing hymns, memorizing verses, and secretly dreaming that someday God would also keep a different story in store for me.

I liked dyeing my hair, even though some people gave me strange looks for it. It was my small act of rebellion, of beauty, of self-affirmation in the middle of so many limitations. That color in my hair reminded me that I too could shine, even if it was only a brief spark in the middle of the gray routine.

I remember that Sunday vividly. Something felt different from the start. I sat in my usual pew, near the aisle, and suddenly I saw him.

Ron.

It wasn't the first time he'd come to church—I'd seen him for years at youth services—but that morning I looked at him differently. Or maybe it was his eyes that looked at me in a way they never had before.

He was sitting on the other side, next to his mother. He dressed with quiet elegance: a white shirt perfectly ironed, dark pants, shoes that shone as if they were new every day. His posture was upright, as if carrying the weight of a strict upbringing. He had that presence that made everyone notice him, but what caught me was the way his eyes searched. It was as if he were looking beyond the sermon, beyond the walls, as if he longed for something he didn't yet have.

When the choir began to sing, our eyes met. I immediately lowered mine, my heart hammering inside my chest. My cheeks burned, and I pressed my little purse against my lap as if I could hide behind it.

The sermon was about faith as small as a mustard seed. I listened, and at the same time, I didn't. Every time I dared to lift my gaze, I found his eyes back on me, and it left me defenseless.

When the service ended, people began greeting each other, sharing comments about the sermon, laughing with old friends. I stayed in my seat, pretending to look for something in my purse. In reality, I just needed to breathe and calm my nerves.

That's when I felt it—a shadow leaning over me, a low, polite voice:

"Excuse me… is this seat taken?"

I looked up, and there he was. Ron. Standing with a shy smile that softened his confident presence.

I froze for a few seconds, then quickly shook my head.

"Thanks," he said, sitting down—even though the service was already over and most people were leaving.

We didn't speak further. He seemed like he wanted to say something, but didn't. I toyed with the comb in my purse, begging my heart to quiet down. For anyone else, it might have been an insignificant moment. But for me, it was the beginning of something I didn't yet know how to name.

That afternoon, I didn't want to go straight home. The air was warm, and the sky was blue, inviting me to walk. I crossed the park in front of the church, where kids kicked around worn-out balls and old men gathered to talk about politics.

There was an empty bench, half-hidden under a large tree. I sat there, letting the breeze tousle my hair. I closed my eyes for a moment and prayed silently, asking God to help me understand why my heart was beating differently.

Not ten minutes later, I heard footsteps. I opened my eyes—and there he was again.

"Mind if I sit?" he asked, with the same unexpected courtesy.

I didn't know what to say. I just nodded.

He sat beside me, leaving a respectful space, as if afraid to disturb me. For a while, neither of us spoke. The rustle of the leaves and the laughter of children filled the silence.

Finally, he sighed.

"I always come here after service. I like to think... no one interrupts me here."

"I come here too," I whispered. "It's peaceful."

He turned toward me, and once again our eyes met. His gaze held honesty—and something else: a tenderness I wasn't expecting.

"I've seen you many times," he said at last. "But today... I don't know. Today I couldn't stop looking at you."

My heart leapt. I felt my face flush, and I lowered my eyes to the ground.

"You shouldn't say that..." I murmured, though deep down I longed to hear it again and again.

"I know. But it's the truth," he answered softly.

I stayed quiet, battling the storm of emotions inside me. It was impossible. We came from different worlds. He was the son of a powerful man; I was just the daughter of a woman

19

who cleaned houses. And yet, there we were, sharing a bench in the park, as if nothing else existed.

The conversation was short, interrupted by the church bells signaling the close of the afternoon. We stood almost at the same time. He walked a few steps with me, then stopped and gave a respectful farewell.

"Until next Sunday," he said—and those words carved themselves into my heart like a promise.

I walked home with a lighter soul, as if I had discovered a beautiful secret. Yet as I went, I couldn't shake the feeling that someone had been watching us. A figure lingered at the edge of the park, staring. I couldn't make out who it was, or if it was even real. Maybe it was just my imagination.

Or maybe not.

That night, as I lay in bed, I stroked my dyed hair and pressed the little New Testament from my purse against my chest. I sighed—half in fear, half in hope. I didn't know what was coming, but something inside me whispered that my life would never be the same again.

CHAPTER 2

WHISPERS IN THE SHADOWS

I thought I could hide it. I truly believed that what had happened on that park bench, those glances, that brief conversation with Ron, could remain my secret. Something only God and I knew.

But secrets have wings. And in a neighborhood like mine, where walls are thin and windows wide open, even the smallest sigh can travel faster than the wind.

At first, it was just a feeling—a look from the women at church, the way someone's voice would drop to a whisper when I walked past. I told myself it was my imagination, but deep down I knew it wasn't. Something had changed.

By Tuesday, on my way to the little grocery store, I heard it clearly. Two neighbors were talking at the corner, one of them holding a basket of tomatoes. They didn't see me coming.

"They say she dyed her hair again. You know what that means."

"She's looking for attention. And not from just anyone. From *him*."

A giggle followed, sharp as broken glass.

I walked faster, clutching the few coins in my pocket. My face burned, not from shame but from the heavy weight of their words pressing against my back.

At night, lying in bed, I tried to convince myself it didn't matter. That people always talk, and tomorrow they'd find someone else to whisper about. But it wasn't true. Every word stuck to me like dust, and I couldn't shake it off.

I prayed longer than usual, asking God for strength. I told Him I didn't want to fall into pride or foolishness. I only wanted to be faithful. But even as I prayed, Ron's smile appeared in my memory, and I didn't know if that was my temptation... or my answer.

Sunday came again. My hands trembled as I tied my hair with the little ribbon I used when I wanted to look "respectable." I chose the same blouse as always—the only nice one I had.

At church, the air felt heavy. I could almost hear the whispers bouncing against the wooden pews. But when I saw him—Ron—standing near the door, waiting, the noise around me faded. His eyes lit up when they met mine, and for a moment, it felt like the whole world was on our side.

During the sermon, I couldn't focus. Not on the verses, not on the pastor's words. My heart was caught in the storm of fear and longing. I knew that after the service, he'd try to speak to me again. And I also knew there would be eyes watching.

And indeed, when we stepped out into the courtyard, he approached me. He was careful, leaving just enough space between us to keep appearances, but his voice was soft enough that only I could hear.

"Can I see you later?"

I hesitated. Everything inside me screamed that it was dangerous, that the murmurs were already spreading, that if I said yes, it would only get worse.

But then I looked into his eyes, and I remembered the peace of sitting with him under that tree, the way my heart had found a new rhythm just by being near him.

I nodded.

"Where?" I whispered.

"The park. Same bench."

That afternoon, the park felt different. The children's laughter seemed distant, the breeze heavier, the sunlight sharper. I sat waiting, twisting my fingers around the strap of my little purse.

When he finally arrived, I breathed again. He smiled, a mixture of relief and determination, and sat beside me.

We didn't speak for a long time. Words seemed unnecessary. Our silence was full of meaning, and yet fragile, as if one wrong word could shatter everything.

Finally, he leaned closer, not enough for anyone to suspect, but enough for me to feel the warmth of his presence.

"Esther," he said softly, "I don't know what's happening to me. But I can't stop thinking about you."

My breath caught. No one had ever said my name like that before, with such tenderness, as if it were a secret prayer.

"Ron..." I whispered, but the rest of my words dissolved.

He reached for my hand, barely brushing it with his fingers, a fleeting touch, yet powerful enough to make my heart race.

"I don't care what people say," he continued, his voice steady. "I don't care about their looks or their whispers. I just want to be where you are."

Tears welled in my eyes. Because I cared. I cared about the whispers, the looks, the wagging tongues. But I also knew that if I walked away from him now, something inside me would die.

"I don't want to be the cause of trouble," I said at last, my voice trembling.

"You're not," he answered firmly. "The trouble is theirs. Not ours."

That evening, as the sun sank and painted the park golden, we finally stood. He didn't try to hold me. He didn't need to. Just before leaving, he whispered again:

"Next Sunday."

And with those words, he left, walking with the calm assurance of someone who had already made his choice.

I stayed behind, clutching my little purse, my heart torn between fear and hope. The murmurs would grow louder, I knew it. The shadows were already gathering.

But so was the light.

And deep inside, I already knew: I wouldn't be able to turn back.

CHAPTER 3
SILENT PROMISES

That week felt endless. Every day I woke up with the memory of Ron's voice still echoing inside me, as if he had whispered my name while I slept. I carried that secret with me everywhere: while helping my mother hang laundry, while waiting in line at the market, while bowing my head in prayer at night.

And yet, the whispers didn't stop. They multiplied. Like weeds sprouting after the rain, they seemed to come from every corner of the neighborhood. I pretended not to hear, but the words reached me anyway.

"She thinks she's better than us, just because he looks at her."

"Doesn't she know where she comes from? Poor girl, she'll only get hurt."

"She won't last long. The son of Emilio isn't for the likes of her."

I tried to harden myself, to let their words bounce off me, but sometimes they pierced deeper than I wanted to admit. And yet... whenever I closed my eyes, I saw his smile. Whenever I remembered his words—*Next Sunday*—my heart leapt with a mixture of fear and longing.

That Sunday, I dressed carefully. My blouse was ironed, my skirt neatly brushed, my hair tied back but with just enough of the dyed strands showing. It was the best I could do.

When I entered the church, I felt it immediately. The glances, the silent nudges, the quick whispers. My steps faltered for a second, but then I saw him.

Ron.

He was waiting near the back pew, and when our eyes met, his expression softened. It was as if nothing else in the world mattered—only that I had walked in.

The service began. Hymns filled the air, verses were read, the pastor preached about perseverance. I heard the words, but more than anything, I heard the rhythm of my own heart. The knowledge that, after the service, we would steal another moment together gave me both strength and trembling anticipation.

When the service ended, people filed out slowly, lingering in groups. I stayed back, pretending to rearrange my little purse. I didn't have to look; I felt him approach.

"Can you meet me?" His voice was low, urgent.

I nodded without daring to turn my head.

"After sundown. The park."

He walked away before anyone could notice. My pulse throbbed in my ears.

That evening, the park glowed under the last rays of sunlight. I walked quickly, holding my purse tight against my side. I chose the same bench under the large tree, my heart racing faster with every step.

When he arrived, everything around me faded. His presence was enough to quiet the noise inside me. He sat close—closer than before, though still careful.

"Thank you for coming," he said, and there was relief in his voice, as if he had been afraid I wouldn't.

"I almost didn't," I confessed softly. "People are talking. They say things that…"

"I know," he interrupted, his jaw tightening. "I've heard them too. But listen to me—none of that matters. Not to me."

His eyes were burning, steady, unwavering.

"Ron," I whispered, "you don't understand. Their words stick to me. I hear them everywhere. They're louder than my own thoughts sometimes."

He leaned forward, so close I could feel the warmth of his breath.

"Then let my words be louder," he said. "Let what I feel for you be stronger than their noise."

I froze, trembling, caught between fear and something so tender it almost hurt.

That night, as the moon rose over the park, we lingered longer than we should have. He spoke of his dreams, of how suffocating it was to live under the shadow of his father's expectations. I spoke of my mother, of the small joys and quiet burdens of my life.

For the first time, it felt like our two worlds weren't so far apart. As if, sitting on that bench, we were equals.

When it was time to go, he touched my hand again. This time, he didn't pull away so quickly. His fingers lingered over mine, trembling, hesitant, but full of unspoken promises.

"Next Sunday," he whispered again, and it sounded less like a question and more like a vow.

I walked home with tears threatening my eyes, not from sadness but from the fragile beauty of what was beginning.

And yet, as I turned the corner of my street, I felt it again—the weight of a gaze, the chill of being watched. I spun around, but the street was empty, only shadows stretching long in the lamplight.

Still, I knew it in my bones: someone had seen us.

And whispers... whispers never stay quiet for long.

CHAPTER 4

THE SHADOW IN THE PARK

The following days carried a strange weight, as if time itself had slowed down. I went about my chores, I laughed with my sister, I even sang while helping my mother, but deep inside, everything was different. There was a pulse beneath the ordinary, a secret rhythm only I could hear. It was the thought of him.

And yet, the whispers grew stronger. This time they weren't just vague comments overheard at the market or muttered outside the church. They became sharper, pointed, as if someone wanted me to feel them cut.

"She's making a fool of herself."

"Doesn't she realize he's just passing the time?"

"Soon she'll learn her place."

I pretended not to care, but each word lodged itself like a thorn under my skin. I prayed at night, asking God to give me strength, to remind me who I was beyond their voices. And still... I waited for Sunday with a heart that beat louder than my doubts.

That Sunday, the church felt smaller, heavier. Every glance burned against my back as I walked down the aisle to my usual seat. I wanted to disappear, but when I saw him, everything else faded.

Ron was there. His eyes found mine, steady, reassuring. He didn't smile—not fully—but there was a softness in his gaze that told me: *I see you. You are not alone.*

The sermon spoke of trials and perseverance. I listened with all my senses, as if each word was meant to prepare me for something I could not yet name.

After the service, he didn't approach me in the open. Instead, as people crowded toward the doors, I felt the faintest brush of his hand against mine. It was fleeting, almost accidental, but in that instant I knew what it meant: *Later.*

The park was quiet that evening. Too quiet.

The laughter of children, so common on Sundays, was gone. The breeze moved through the trees, stirring their branches, but the place felt strangely deserted. I walked slowly, each step echoing in my chest.

When I reached our bench under the tree, he was already there, waiting. He stood when he saw me, his face breaking into a look that was part relief, part longing.

"You came," he said softly.

"I said I would," I replied, though my voice trembled.

We sat. For a while we didn't speak. Silence wrapped around us, heavy but not uncomfortable. Then, he turned toward me, his expression grave.

"There's something I need to tell you," he began. "But you must promise not to be afraid."

My breath caught.

"What is it?" I asked, my fingers twisting nervously in my lap.

He hesitated, his eyes scanning the shadows around us before he leaned closer.

"Someone's been watching us."

A shiver ran down my spine.

"I thought it was just me," I whispered. "I felt it too. Like eycs following me when I leave."

He nodded slowly, his jaw tightening.

"It's not your imagination. I noticed it last Sunday. A figure, always keeping distance, but never too far. Tonight, I think they're here again."

I froze, my heartbeat roaring in my ears. My instinct told me to turn, to look, but his hand reached out and touched mine firmly.

"Don't," he said. "If they know we've seen them, it might get worse."

His touch was warm, steady, and for a fleeting moment, the fear eased.

"Why?" I asked, my voice barely audible. "Why would anyone care?"

He looked at me then, his eyes filled with a mixture of tenderness and sorrow.

"Because they know," he murmured. "They see what I feel for you. And that's enough to make us a threat."

We left the park separately that night, pretending nothing was wrong. But inside, everything had changed.

I walked home quickly, the shadows stretching long on the path ahead. Twice I thought I heard footsteps behind me. Twice I turned, but the street lay empty.

When I finally reached my door, I pressed my back

against the wood and shut my eyes tight, whispering a prayer.

I had found something precious, something fragile and beautiful. But now, I understand: beauty doesn't come without danger.

And the silence around us was beginning to break.

CHAPTER 5

A VOICE IN THE SHADOWS

The days after that night felt like walking with a storm cloud above me. Outwardly, life went on as usual: I helped my mother with her work, laughed with my sister, attended service on Wednesdays and Sundays. But inside, every sound, every step, carried a question: *Is someone watching me now?*

I tried to dismiss the thought, but it was impossible. I'd catch myself turning around in the market, glancing at corners, scanning faces in the street. Maybe it was only paranoia. Or maybe Ron was right—maybe there truly was a shadow trailing us.

Despite the fear, I couldn't stop thinking of him. His words lingered in my heart like a secret flame: *They see what I feel for you.* That confession, whispered under the trees, gave me courage, even as unease pressed on me from all sides.

That Sunday, when I entered the church, my steps faltered. Emilio—the pastor, Ron's father—was at the pulpit already, his eyes sweeping over the congregation like a hawk surveying its prey. He always had that commanding presence, but this time, I felt his gaze linger on me a second too long.

I bowed my head and slipped into my usual seat. My hands trembled slightly as I opened my worn New Testament. I prayed silently, asking God to guard my heart, to give me wisdom.

The sermon was stern, more than usual. Words about obedience, purity, and the dangers of temptation struck the air like heavy stones. It felt less like teaching and more like warning. And though Emilio never mentioned names, my skin prickled with the certainty that he was speaking about me.

Beside him, Ron sat straight, silent, his jaw tense. He didn't look at me, not once. That hurt more than I expected.

After service, I stayed behind, letting the crowd flow out before me. I needed space, a chance to breathe. But just as

I stepped outside, I felt a voice—sharp, low—cut through the noise.

"You should be careful."

I froze.

A man stood a few feet away, half-hidden near the corner of the church. His face was in shadow, his tone dripping with disdain.

"Not everything that shines is meant for you," he said coldly. "Some fires burn what they touch."

Before I could answer, before I could even move, he was gone—slipping into the crowd, leaving me trembling.

Who was he? A church member? A stranger? Or perhaps one of those who whispered in Emilio's ear?

That evening, I returned to the park, though every instinct told me not to. My heart beat hard as I approached the bench under the tree.

Ron was there, waiting, his face drawn with worry.

"You shouldn't have come," he said immediately, standing.

"Neither should you," I answered, though my voice was steadier than I felt.

He looked at me then, anguish in his eyes.

"They're watching us more closely now," he confessed. "My father suspects… and others will try to stop us before he does."

I told him about the voice I'd heard, the shadow near the church. His expression darkened, his fists clenching.

"They won't scare me away," he said firmly. "They can't take this from us."

I wanted to believe him. I wanted his words to be a shield against the fear crawling through me. And yet, deep down, I knew: what we had awakened was no longer just between us.

There were eyes everywhere.

And soon, the silence would shatter.

CHAPTER 6
A REFUGE FOR TWO

After that frightening encounter outside the church, I thought fear would drive me away from Ron. But instead, it drew me closer. It was as if danger itself had become a wall pressing against us, forcing us to seek refuge in each other.

Whenever I felt the weight of eyes on me, or when the whispers of neighbors reached my ears, my heart ran to him. Not with words—those could be overheard—but with longing, with a silent prayer that somehow we would find a way to meet.

And God, in His mysterious mercy, gave us that way.

We started meeting in small, hidden places. Sometimes in the park, but only when the sun was high and people were distracted with their own lives. Sometimes by chance—or so it seemed—on the path that led to the river, where laundrywomen laughed loudly enough to cover our voices.

Each time, our conversations began cautiously, almost whispering, as if the trees themselves could betray us. But little by little, the caution gave way to tenderness.

"Do you ever wish we had met somewhere else?" I asked him once, as we sat under the shade of a tree, my hands clutching the small New Testament in my lap.

He shook his head without hesitation. "No. I believe God wanted us to meet here. Even in the middle of this noise. Even with all this against us."

His conviction amazed me. I had doubts, fears that gnawed at my chest, but when Ron spoke with that steady voice, I felt my soul quiet.

There was one evening when the world outside seemed to blur away.

The day had been unbearably hot, and the sunset poured golden light over the park. I walked quickly, nervous that someone might notice me, but when I saw Ron waiting by the bench, all fear dissolved.

We sat closer than usual. The heat of the day had given

way to a soft breeze, and somehow that made everything feel more intimate, more fragile.

"Sometimes," he admitted, his eyes fixed on the ground, "I wonder if it's selfish of me to keep pulling you into this. I know what people are saying. I know the risks for you."

I reached for his hand before I even realized what I was doing. His fingers tightened around mine as though that small gesture gave him back the strength he had momentarily lost.

"It doesn't feel like a risk," I whispered. "Not when I'm with you. It feels… safe. Like nothing else matters."

He turned to me then, and for a moment I thought he would speak. But he didn't. Instead, his hand lifted, brushing a stray lock of hair from my forehead. The touch was so gentle it felt like a prayer.

That was the moment we both leaned in—hesitant, trembling—and our lips finally met.

The kiss was soft, almost shy, but behind it was all the longing we had been holding back. It felt like stepping into forbidden light, fragile and dangerous, yet impossible to resist.

When we parted, I could hardly breathe. His forehead rested against mine, and I heard him whisper:

"Esther… you're my refuge."

45

Tears burned my eyes. I pressed my hand to his cheek, clinging to the truth of his words, even as I knew the storm around us was only growing stronger.

That night, as I lay in bed, I replayed every second of that kiss. It was reckless, maybe even foolish. But it was also the most sacred thing I had ever known.

For the first time, I understood what it meant for two souls to find shelter in each other—while the world outside sharpened its knives.

CHAPTER 7

THE WEIGHT OF WHISPERS

At first, I thought the rumors would fade, like a brief shadow passing over a sunny day. But shadows lengthen. They spread until the light itself feels smothered.

It started with glances—those sideways looks that sting more than words. A woman at the market paused mid-bargain just to stare at me. A neighbor who once smiled kindly when we crossed paths now pressed her lips together, cold and tight.

I tried to ignore it. I clung to the memory of Ron's hand in mine, to the whisper of his voice calling me his refuge. But every day, it grew harder to pretend.

One morning, as I carried a basket of laundry to the river, two women were already there, scrubbing clothes against the rocks. They lowered their voices when I approached, but not enough.

"She thinks she can climb higher by catching his eye," one muttered.

"And with painted hair, no less. No shame at all," the other replied.

Their words cut deeper than I wanted to admit. I lowered my gaze, knelt by the water, and dipped the fabric into the current. My hands moved mechanically, but my chest burned.

I told myself it didn't matter. People talk. They always talk. But that afternoon, as I returned home with the damp basket balanced against my hip, I passed Rosa—our neighbor, once like an older sister to me.

She stood at her doorway, arms crossed.

"Esther," she called, her voice sharp as a blade.

I stopped, shifting the weight of the basket. "Yes?"

Her eyes traveled over me with something like contempt. "Everyone sees you with him. Do you think it will end well? Do you think his world will ever accept you? You're only making yourself a fool."

I opened my mouth, but no words came. My throat closed, as though her judgment had stolen even the air.

She didn't wait for an answer. She turned back inside, the door slamming like a final verdict.

That night, I couldn't sleep. I lay awake staring at the ceiling, hearing Rosa's words over and over again. *A fool. A fool. A fool.*

But when I closed my eyes, I saw Ron's face, his smile breaking through the shadows. And I knew, despite the ache, that I could not let go.

Still… the weight of whispers was pressing harder every day.

And something inside me feared that soon, the whispers would no longer be enough for those who wanted to see me fall.

CHAPTER 8
FAITH IN THE MIDST OF DESPAIR

There are nights when silence does not comfort—it weighs. That night, after what happened with Rosa, the air felt heavy, as if every shadow slipping through my window carried judgments, rumors, invisible voices whispering how unworthy I was. I tried to sleep, but my heart wouldn't allow it… and the certainty that none of this was over burned inside me.

The next day Ron came to see me. The moment I saw him enter the small living room of our house, I knew he was different… his eyes were aflame, his steps sure, as if he carried a storm inside his chest he could no longer hold back.

"I can't take it anymore, Esther…" he said at once, without even greeting me. "I can't bear them humiliating you, pointing at you as if you were guilty of something…"

His voice broke at the end, not from weakness but from anger. I looked at him, moved and at the same time frightened.

"Ron…" I whispered, stepping closer, "don't say that so loud—someone could hear us."

He gripped my hands tightly.

"And what does it matter? Everyone already knows, everyone is already talking… do you think it frightens me? What hurts me is seeing how they look at you, how they treat you…"

I closed my eyes because his words pierced me like thorns. Yes, it hurt, but more than that I was scared to see him so desperate.

We sat down, and he started pacing back and forth, unable to keep still.

"I've thought about talking to my father directly, confronting him once and for all… telling him I won't leave you, that I don't care what he does or what he says."

I stared at him. His voice was full of fire, but I knew what that fire could cause if it overflowed.

"Ron… if you do that now, it will be worse…" I murmured. "Emilio is not a man who listens calmly… you know that."

He stopped and looked at me, pain obvious in his eyes.

"Then tell me what to do, Esther… because if I stand here with my arms crossed, I feel like I'm losing you…"

I swallowed, breathed deeply, and laid my hand over his chest, feeling his pounding heart.

"You won't lose me..." I said softly. "Not while we stay together, not while we trust..."

He hugged me so hard that I could hardly breathe. It was a desperate embrace, the kind of hug someone gives when fighting an invisible enemy.

"I want to take you far away..." he whispered into my hair, "even if only for a while, even if it must be in secret..."

My heart flipped.

"Ron... don't talk about running away..."

"And what other way out do we have?" he interrupted, pulling back to look me in the eyes. "Here everyone points at you, my father pulls strings against you, the church itself turns its back on you... how long can we stand this?"

A chill ran through me because his words were true, and at the same time I knew that running wasn't the answer... not yet.

I moved aside a little, needing space to breathe.

"Ron, listen... I'm tired too, I feel the weight of all this, but I don't want our desperation to make us lose what we have..."

He looked at me, brow furrowed, as if trying to understand.

"I pray every night," I continued. "I ask God to give us strength, to show us a way… and even though sometimes it feels like He keeps silence, I feel here"—I put my hand to my chest—"that He has not abandoned us…"

Ron lowered his gaze, and for a moment I saw him vulnerable, like a child.

"I want to believe it, Esther… but it gets harder for me every day…"

I stepped closer and cupped his face in my hands.

"Then believe it with me… you don't have to carry that faith alone; I can hold it for both of us when you feel you can't anymore…"

His eyes filled with tears, and something inside me trembled. I had never seen him so fragile.

"You're stronger than you seem…" he murmured in a hoarse voice, "and I… I only want to protect you, even if it breaks me to a thousand pieces."

"And I only want to love you…" I answered, barely above a whisper, "even if the world comes crashing down on us."

We sat in silence, breathing the same air, our foreheads pressed together. Outside, the rumors would continue to grow—I knew that—but in that moment, there the world shrank to the two of us, and amid his desperation and my faith there was an indestructible refuge.

That night, when I found myself alone again, I thought of him and all we had talked about. I remembered his fire, his urge to fight, and I remembered my own fear. And I understood something... that our difference was, in truth, our complement.

He burned to defend me... I held the calm so it wouldn't overflow.

He wanted to shout at the world... I wanted to kneel silently before God.

He was strength... I was hope.

And together, we were love.

I closed my eyes and prayed in silence, stronger than ever. I asked that the faith that sustained me might also reach Ron, filling him with the peace I felt in those few seconds of calm.

Because I knew the worst was still to come... and when that moment arrived, the only thing that could keep us standing would be that invisible union that bound us — beyond rumors, beyond fears, beyond Emilio's rage.

And while the wind blew outside with its constant murmur, I repeated over and over in my mind, as if these were the words that kept me breathing:

"We are not alone... we are not alone..."

CHAPTER 9

THE STORM BREAKS

The air that afternoon was heavy, weighed down by a strange silence that seemed to foretell something. I walked beside Ron, moving slowly across the square after the church service. He had insisted on accompanying me, even though he knew every stare would pierce us like darts.

And yes, they were there—the eyes of half the neighborhood following us, whispers slithering like snakes between benches and trees. Heat rushed to my face, but at the same time, his hand in mine was a shield against it all.

"Don't be afraid," he said softly. "We owe them nothing…"

I nodded, though my heart pounded so loudly it felt like everyone could hear it.

We stopped near the fountain, under the shade of an almond tree. Ron looked at me with that intensity that made me forget the noise all around.

"Esther... no matter what happens, I won't leave you."

I smiled at him, though my eyes shone with tears.

"Nor I you... even if the whole world stands against us."

It was in that moment, when I felt we could defy the universe itself, that the thunderous voice split our souls in two.

"What is the meaning of this?!"

I turned and saw him. Emilio. His imposing figure cut against the fading light, his eyes blazing with fury. His firm steps shook the ground, and behind him, neighbors gathered quickly, drawn by the spectacle.

My breath caught. Ron instantly moved in front of me like a wall, but Emilio was already only a few steps away.

"So it's true!" he roared. "Not just rumors, not just gossip... you rub it in my face, in the middle of the square!"

Curious eyes pierced us, expectant, hungry for blood. I wanted to sink into the earth.

"Father..." Ron began, his voice firm but his hands trembling, "don't speak like that—"

"Silence!" Emilio cut him off, raising his hand as if slicing the air. "What disgrace is this? You, my son, with this girl?"

I closed my eyes. His words cut through me, each syllable a blow. *This girl.* He didn't even call me by my name.

Ron stepped forward, still holding my hand.

"Her name is Esther. And I love her."

The murmur of the crowd rose like a restrained roar. Emilio paled, but his lips twisted into a sneer.

"Love? Don't make me laugh!" he spat. "This is a whim, a madness… she clings to you because of what you have, because she wants to take advantage."

I lowered my head, tears burning my eyes. The ground shifted beneath me, each word stripping away pieces of my dignity.

"No!" Ron shouted, his voice cracking with fury. "Don't you dare speak of her that way! Esther is not what you say. She is purer, more sincere than anyone here judging us today."

Emilio took another step, so close I could feel his breath, thick with rage.

"You defy me, son? Me? For her?"

The silence of the neighbors was unbearable. All eyes were on us—some with morbid curiosity, others with pity, others with indignation. I spotted Rosa among them, her stern expression tightening my throat.

But Ron did not back down.

"Yes, I defy you… because I will not leave her."

Emilio's face hardened even more.

"If you continue with this, forget being my son. Forget my name, my house, my support. You'll be left with nothing."

I gasped, squeezing Ron's hand. I wanted to beg him to stay quiet, not to answer, not to put me on a scale against his father. But when I looked at him, I knew there was no turning back.

"Then I'll be left with nothing," Ron said firmly. "But with her."

The square erupted in murmurs. I felt the air leave my lungs. Emilio's face reddened, his contained fury on the verge of breaking loose.

"Ungrateful!" he roared. "You're blinded! And you—" he pointed at me with a finger like a knife—"you are the cause of this. You've poisoned my son with your tricks, but I swear you will not destroy my family."

I trembled, torn between answering or fleeing. I wanted to speak, to say it wasn't true, that I sought nothing—but my voice was trapped in my throat.

Ron stepped in front of me again, a living shield.

"Don't blame her. If you must blame someone, blame me. I sought her out, I chose her, and I would choose her a thousand times more."

The crowd held its breath. Every word was a blade thrown in public, every reply another crack in the wall Emilio had built between us.

He looked me up and down with scorn.

"Girl... you have no idea what you've gotten yourself into. I won't rest until you disappear from his life."

A sob broke from me. Ron pulled me into his arms, holding me tight in front of everyone, a defiant embrace.

"Then you'll have to go through me," he told his father, his voice icy calm. "Because Esther and I... we won't hide anymore."

The murmurs burst like a flooded river. Some walked away, indignant, others lingered to see how the drama would end. Emilio breathed heavily, his gaze filled with hate, until at last he spat the words like venom:

"This isn't over. You'll regret it."

He turned and stormed away, leaving behind a frozen silence.

I remained trembling in Ron's arms, unable to stand on my own. Tears streamed freely down my face, but amid the pain, there was something else: a certainty.

The storm had finally broken.

There were no more rumors, no more half-truths. Now it was open war.

And though I was terrified, I knew I wasn't alone.

Because Ron held me, and in the deepest part of my heart, I felt God would too.

CHAPTER 10

ESTHER'S BREAKING POINT

I will never forget the weight of those stares, the muffled voices, the whispers that turned into knives in the air. From that day in the square, when Emilio caught us in front of everyone, I felt something inside me shatter... like a fragile glass smashed against the floor, impossible to piece back together.

I kept telling myself I had to be strong, to lean on the love Ron had shown me. But every time I closed my eyes, I saw Emilio's voice raised in fury, the neighbors whispering, Rosa's twisted smile of triumph. The echo of it all lodged in my chest like a thorn I couldn't pull out.

That night I couldn't sleep. I tossed in bed, crying silently so my mother wouldn't hear. My pillow was soaked, and I felt as though the whole world had pressed me against the wall. I was afraid. Afraid of losing him, afraid he would give in to his father's pressure, afraid the rumors would swell so big they'd suffocate me.

And yet, somewhere in the midst of all that, a corner of my heart refused to give in. I slipped from bed to my knees, hands trembling, and whispered with barely a voice:

"Lord… I don't understand what You're doing. I don't understand why this love, which feels so pure, has become a source of pain and rejection. But I ask You to hold me. Don't let me fall. Don't let me go."

The tears kept running, but inside I felt something—like a soft peace, a thin invisible thread assuring me I wasn't alone.

The next day Aunt Lorena came to visit. She has always been blunt, never one to circle around the truth. The moment she saw me, she caught the redness in my eyes and the weariness in my voice. She didn't wait for me to speak. She pulled me into the kitchen, let out a long sigh, and began:

"Sweetheart, I already know what happened yesterday. The whole neighborhood's talking."

A lump rose in my throat. I couldn't meet her eyes.

"Esther," she went on, her hands resting on the table,

64

"you know I love you. I want to see you happy. But this thing you're doing..." Her voice faltered, as if it pained her. "This could ruin your life."

I looked up, startled.

"Ruin my life? Auntie, I love him. And he loves me."

"Yes, yes, I know that's how you feel. But men like him—" she lifted a trembling finger—"they never marry girls like us. And with a father as powerful and proud as Emilio? He'll never let you be with his son. And if he sets his mind to it... he'll crush you."

Her words cut through me like arrows.

"So what then? I should just give up?" My voice rose without meaning to, breaking at the end. "I should pretend my heart doesn't matter?"

She sighed and brushed her hand gently across my cheek, tender yet sorrowful.

"Sometimes, sweetheart, there are loves that bring nothing but pain. And you have to be strong enough to let go before it hurts more."

I went speechless. It was as if the ground opened beneath my feet.

When Ron came to see me that afternoon, my aunt's words were still echoing in my head. He arrived nervous, his shirt wrinkled, eyes burning like he hadn't slept at all. The moment he saw me, he seized my hands.

"Esther, we have to do something," he said bluntly. "My father won't stop. I know him. He'll move heaven and earth to tear us apart."

I swallowed hard, my heart racing.

"I know... but what can we do?"

"I've thought about talking to the pastor. Maybe he could mediate. Or even leaving—do you understand? Finding a place where no one can interfere."

My eyes widened.

"Leave? Ron, that's... that's impossible."

"Nothing is impossible," he said, gripping my hands tighter. "I won't let my father decide for me. I won't let anyone else, either."

Tears welled again. I loved him with everything in me, but there was something in his gaze that frightened me—that mix of rage and desperation. It burned like a fire out of control.

I wrapped my arms around him, pressing my head to his chest.

"Ron... I only know this: whatever happens, we can't lose our faith. That's the one thing that can hold us up."

He stroked my hair but said nothing. And in his silence, I felt his struggle: torn between his love for me and the hatred rising against his father.

That night I prayed again. This time with more tears, my voice trembling.

"Lord... I don't want to hate. I don't want pain to consume us. Guard Ron's heart. Don't let his anger carry him away. Don't let him lose sight of who You are in the middle of this storm."

And for a moment, in the silence of the night, it felt as though my words hadn't vanished into the void—as though Someone up above truly heard me.

But the calm didn't last. Two days later, while walking through the market with a loaf of bread under my arm, I overheard two women whispering. They didn't notice I was near.

"Poor girl, so caught up in her illusions," said one.

"Illusions? Please," the other sneered. "That girl knows exactly what she's doing. She's after Ron's money. Haven't you seen the way she clings to him?"

The bread nearly slipped from my hands. I kept walking, head down, my cheeks burning with shame. Every word stung like a thorn.

When I got home, I locked myself in my room and wept

until there was nothing left. And in the middle of my sobs, the only thing that kept me from collapsing was repeating over and over:

"God is with me. God is with me. Even if everyone rejects me, He won't let me go."

Ron came again that evening, more restless than ever.

"Esther," he burst out, almost breathless, "my father's been speaking to families in the church. He wants them to shut you out, to bar you from everything. He wants to isolate you."

My soul cracked inside me.

"So… it's begun."

He slammed his fist on the table, furious.

"I won't allow it! If he dares humiliate you, if he lays a hand on you, if he tries to destroy you—I…"

I threw my arms around him before he could finish, tears rushing to my eyes.

"Ron, no… don't let rage consume you. All we have is our love—and our faith. If we lose that, we lose everything."

He held me against his chest, breathing hard. And in that embrace I felt the two forces that bound us: his desperation and my clinging to God. It was like being in the same boat, tossed by the storm, each of us rowing in a different way.

That night, before sleep, I knelt once more. My aunt's

warning, the rumors, Emilio's fury—all of it weighed on me. Yet in the midst of my prayer, I felt a certainty:

The world may reject me. Even my own family may doubt me. But if God holds me, I will not fall.

I wiped my tears, breathed deep, and went to bed with a single thought in my heart:

The storm is only just beginning… but I am not alone.

CHAPTER 11
PUBLIC HUMILIATION AT CHURCH

The church had always been my refuge. Even when rumors chased me around the neighborhood, when Rosa whispered cruel things behind my back, or when Emilio threw those looks of disdain my way, I found in those white-painted walls a breath of relief, a peace unlike anything else.

Walking through its doors felt like coming home. The murmur of hymns, the smell of old wooden pews, the dim flicker of candles… all of it gave me strength to keep going.

But that morning, as I prepared to sing with the choir like every Sunday, I sensed something different in the air. Quick glances, whispers that went silent the moment I passed, uneasy gestures. I tried to ignore them, to keep my focus on the hymnal in my hands, but a heavy premonition pressed against my chest.

Ron sat in the last pew, arms crossed, his jaw tight. He looked at me as if he already knew what was about to happen.

The pastor had barely finished the opening prayer when a loud, commanding voice shook the sanctuary:

— "Wait a moment!"

The echo made every head turn. Emilio stood in the center aisle, elegant as always, his suit immaculate, his face hardened. He walked to the front with steady steps, as if he were the one leading the service.

A chill ran down my spine. My hands began to tremble, and the hymnal almost slipped from my fingers.

— "With all due respect, Pastor," Emilio said, though his tone carried no respect at all, "before we continue this service, something must be made clear before the entire congregation."

Silence fell over the room. Only the creak of the wooden floorboards under his steps could be heard.

He looked straight at me, his gaze like a dagger.

— "This young woman," he declared, pointing at me, "has no right to be here, standing as if she represented the purity of our faith."

A ripple of murmurs swept across the sanctuary. I felt as though the ground beneath me was splitting open.

— "She," Emilio continued, his voice growing louder,

"has intruded upon my family, tempting my son, dragging him down a crooked path. And I will not allow it."

My heart pounded so loudly I thought everyone must hear it.

—"Enough, Father!" Ron's voice cut through the silence from the back. He rose from his seat and strode quickly toward us. "You have no right to humiliate her like this!"

Emilio shot him a glare sharp enough to wound, but carried on, dismissing his son's protest.

—"Pastor, I demand that this girl never again step up to the choir, nor take part in any church activity. If she wishes to attend, let her sit and listen… but only as a spectator. Nothing more."

His words struck me like a bucket of ice water. I froze, clutching my chest, aware of every pair of eyes fixed on me.

Ron moved to stand directly in front of me, placing himself between his father and me.

—"She's done nothing wrong!" he shouted, his voice burning with fury. "The only thing she's guilty of is loving me! Since when is love a sin?"

Emilio's face darkened further.

—"Loving you?" He let out a bitter laugh. "That isn't love, son. That is manipulation. This girl seeks only to take advantage of you—of us."

I couldn't bear it any longer. My cheeks burned, and tears blurred my vision.

— "That's not true!" I cried, my voice breaking. "I have never wanted anything from your family... all I've ever done is love him, with all my heart."

A heavy silence fell over the congregation. Some lowered their eyes. Others whispered among themselves. The pastor looked trapped, caught in the middle of a storm he couldn't control.

Ron's voice rang out, strong and unshaken:

— "Father, you have no right to decide for me. Nor to destroy Esther's reputation in front of everyone."

Emilio stepped closer, every muscle in his body taut with fury.

— "I am your father. And as long as you live under my roof, you will follow my rules. You will not see her again!"

My heart stopped. My knees shook so hard I thought I might collapse.

Ron met his father's eyes, and in them I saw a fire I had rarely witnessed.

— "Then I will no longer live under your roof."

A strangled murmur rippled through the sanctuary, as if the whole congregation had held its breath at once.

Emilio's face flushed crimson with rage.

— "You are making a mistake, Ron. And she will be your downfall."

I wanted to speak, to defend him, but the words stuck in my throat. All I could do was cling to Ron when he reached for my hand, holding it firmly before everyone, unafraid, defying his father's authority.

That simple gesture, so small yet so powerful, gave me strength.

— "I am not his downfall," I said, tears streaming down my face. "If you let me, I will be his refuge. And he will be mine."

Some exchanged uneasy glances. Others offered faint, secret smiles, as if deep down they recognized our words as truth. But Emilio remained unmoved.

— "This is not over," he growled, his voice low and dangerous. "You will regret this."

He turned and walked out of the church, leaving behind a silence heavier than any sermon.

When it was over, the pastor tried to resume the service, but the atmosphere was shattered. My body trembled uncontrollably. Ron held me close, whispering in my ear:

— "You're not alone. You never will be."

And though shame burned inside me, though it felt

as if Emilio had torn my soul apart before everyone, one certainty glowed within me:

The love that bound us was stronger than any humiliation.

But deep in my heart, I also knew Emilio would not rest until he destroyed us.

That night, in my room, I knelt on shaking knees.

— "Lord… I cannot bear this. But You can. Give me the strength to endure. Don't let hatred consume me. And please… protect him."

The prayer slipped from my lips like a sob, a desperate cry. And in the middle of my fragility, I felt once more that gentle peace, like a whisper saying:

"Do not fear. I am with you."

I clung to that invisible voice, because it was the only thing keeping me standing.

CHAPTER 12

SECRETS AND HIDDEN HOPE

The days after that humiliation at church felt like an endless desert. Silence became my constant companion, and the neighbors' stares, my jailers. No one said anything to me directly, yet every step I took through the neighborhood was followed by whispers that dissolved the moment I turned around.

The worst punishment, however, was not the gossip. It was Ron's absence.

His voice, his laughter, his hands tangled with mine... all of it had vanished in an instant.

It felt as if he had been torn away from me, as if Emilio had finally achieved what he'd always wanted: to separate us not just physically, but deep within our souls.

Each night I cried myself to sleep, clutching my pillow, asking God why He allowed me to endure such pain. Each morning I woke up hoping to see Ron at the corner, or to hear his secret whistle from the plaza… but nothing came. Only emptiness.

His absence weighed heavier than all the humiliations combined.

The rumors grew crueler with each passing day. *"Emilio has locked him away." "They won't let him out of the house anymore." "They're preparing him to be engaged to someone of his own class."*

Every phrase stabbed me like a thorn.

I imagined Ron trapped in that house that looked like a palace but was really a prison. I imagined him desperate, pounding on doors, shouting that he wanted to see me. And even if those visions were nothing but my imagination, I couldn't stop feeling him close—like somehow, his thoughts still searched for me, even if the world tried to tear us apart.

One afternoon, as I returned from the market carrying a small bag of fruit, someone called my name in a low voice from a side alley.

—"Esther!"

I spun around. It was Mateo, his cap pulled low over his

78

forehead, his eyes darting nervously as if to make sure no one had followed him.

I approached with caution, my heart pounding in my throat.

— "What is it?"

He drew in a deep breath, like someone about to commit a forbidden act. Then he reached into his jacket pocket and pulled out a folded envelope.

— "It's from Ron."

I stared at him, unable to react. My fingers trembled as I reached for it.

— "Re... really?"

— "Really," he said firmly, nodding. "He asked me to give it to you in secret. Emilio watches him closely, but he managed to write this in hiding."

A knot rose in my throat, tears burning in my eyes.

— "Thank you, Mateo... you have no idea what this means to me."

He gave me a small smile, as though he understood more than his words revealed.

— "Just... be careful. No one can know."

I nodded quickly, pressing the envelope against my chest, as if it had already become part of me.

I ran home. Locked myself in my room, closed the

window, drew the curtains, and sat on my bed with the envelope in my hands.

I was afraid to open it, as if the moment I did, the paper would crumble and with it the only thread that still tied me to Ron.

Taking a deep breath, wiping the tears from my face, I finally broke the seal.

His handwriting was hurried, slanted, as if his heart had been racing through his fingers.

And then, I read:

*"My beloved Esther,

If these words reach your hands, it means there is still a bridge between us. My father believes he can chain me, but he doesn't know that my heart is already yours, and no key can unlock it without your consent.

These days have been unbearable without you. They watch me, confine me, tell me to forget you, but every second away from you is like dying slowly.

I will not give up. I never will. Even if they try to extinguish what we feel, this love is a fire that cannot be put out.

Esther, please, hold on. Hold tight to our faith, to what we both know is real. I will fight, I promise you. I don't know how or when, but I will be with you again.

You are my refuge, my strength, my reason for everything.

Forever yours,

Ron."

Tears streamed down my cheeks as my lips trembled, rereading every word. I pressed the letter against my heart, holding it as if I were holding Ron himself.

It was his voice that echoed in my mind, his eyes shining in every line, his presence wrapping around me in that silent room.

For the first time in days, my tears were not only of pain, but of relief. He was still there. He had not surrendered.

I knelt beside my bed, the letter still clutched in my hands.

—"Thank You, Lord," I whispered, my heart pounding. "Thank You for not leaving him alone. For not leaving me alone. Give me the strength to wait, to endure. And please... protect him."

A gentle warmth spread through me, as if heaven itself were holding me in an invisible embrace.

I placed the letter inside my Bible, between the pages of a psalm that spoke of refuge in the midst of the storm.

Every time I touched it, it felt like touching his hand.

Every time I read it, I could hear his voice whispering in my ear.

The world could say we were separated, that Emilio had won, that I was defeated... but within me burned one certainty: our love was still alive, hidden within those words on a wrinkled page.

And as long as love remained, there would always be hope.

CHAPTER 13

THE STORM BREAKS

The silence of the night embraced me like a heavy cloak. Outside, the voices of the neighborhood had already faded, and only the distant crow of a rooster, too early for dawn, broke the stillness. In my hands, Ron's letter had become almost an extension of my skin: I pulled it from its hiding place over and over again, as if my eyes could not believe what they had already read a thousand times.

"I won't give up. I never will."

That phrase echoed like a drum in my heart. And suddenly, I understood: I couldn't give up either. Emilio could build walls, use his power and money like chains, try to erase me from Ron's world... but what we felt was stronger than all of that.

I knelt by the bed, as I did every night, but my prayers had changed. They were no longer just tearful pleas, no longer questions thrown at the sky. That night, I prayed with a steady voice, eyes closed and tears flowing freely, but with a fire inside me that would not go out:

—*Lord, do not let this love die. If it comes from You, protect it. Give me strength, because I know the greatest storm is still ahead.*

And yes, the storm came.

The next day, in the plaza, I heard a murmur louder than usual. Several women were gathered near the fountain, and as I passed by with my basket, I felt their gazes stab into me like knives. One of them, Rosa—the most venomous of all—muttered loudly:

—*Poor boy... they say Emilio keeps him like a prisoner, all because of that little girl who doesn't know her place.*

Another one laughed with irony.

—*It's just a passing fever. In the end, blood and money always win.*

I kept walking with my head held high, but inside I trembled. I wanted to answer, to shout that it wasn't a whim, that it wasn't a game... but I stayed silent. Because I knew Ron's words, kept in my chest, were worth more than all those rumors.

That same afternoon, Mateo appeared again. This time he brought no letter, only a worried face.

—*Esther, you need to be prepared*, he said quietly, walking at my side. *Emilio is angrier than ever. Ron argued with him last night, and they almost came to blows.*

I froze.

—*What?*

Mateo nodded seriously.

—*Ron told him he wasn't going to forget you, that he wouldn't stop fighting. Emilio lost control, he shouted like I'd never seen him before. And now... now he wants to take it further.*

The air caught in my lungs.

—*Further how?*

Mateo swallowed hard, as if he didn't want to say it.

—*He wants to drive you out of the church. He wants to make sure there's no place where you and Ron can meet. He says he's going to speak with the pastor in front of everyone.*

The ground beneath my feet felt unstable. The church was my refuge, the only place where I could still breathe without feeling like a shadow. And now he wanted to take even that away from me?

—*No...* I whispered, lips trembling. *He can't do that to me.*

Mateo looked at me with sorrow.

—*With Emilio, never say "he can't."*

Sunday arrived like a sentence.

I dressed in my simple skirt and white blouse, and though I tried to stay calm, my hands would not stop sweating. With the Bible in my bag and Ron's letter hidden between its pages, I walked toward the church. Every step felt like it could be the last I ever took inside that place.

The church was full. The murmur of the congregation floated in the air, and the choir was tuning their voices in a corner. I found a seat in the back pew, hoping to go unnoticed… but I could feel the stares. Judging eyes. Pitying eyes. Curious eyes, hungry for scandal.

And then I saw him. Emilio, standing beside the pastor, tall and proud, his brow darkened with a frown. Behind him, Ron. His gaze found mine instantly. His father's hand gripped his shoulder, but his eyes screamed the words his lips could not: *I am with you.*

My heart pounded so hard I thought everyone must hear it.

The pastor raised his voice, calling for silence. The congregation settled. Emilio stepped forward. His shadow stretched across the altar, dark, commanding.

—*Today I have something to say.*

The hush grew heavy, suffocating. I swallowed hard, my stomach tightening.

—*My son,* Emilio continued, pointing at Ron, *has fallen into error. An error I will not allow to ruin his life, nor the good name of our community.*

I felt the blood freeze in my veins.

—*That girl,* he spat, and his eyes locked on me like daggers, *will never set foot in this church again.*

A ripple of shock swept through the sanctuary. The pastor shifted uneasily, but Emilio gave him no chance to speak.

I sat paralyzed, throat dry, clutching the Bible tight against my chest.

And then it happened.

Ron wrenched free of his father's grip and stepped forward. His voice rang out, stronger than I had ever heard it.

—*No!*

The word echoed through the church, bold and unshaken, bouncing off the walls like thunder. The congregation gasped; some even turned to one another in disbelief.

I couldn't breathe. Between fear and hope, my heart was suspended in midair.

Ron moved another step closer, trembling, but his eyes locked firmly on his father.

—*I will not allow you to humiliate Esther like this.*

A hymnbook slipped from someone's hands; a whispered "Oh, my God" floated through the room.

Emilio turned on him, livid, face flushed, fists clenched.

—*What did you just say?*

—*You heard me,* Ron shot back, his voice steady. *I love Esther. And I will not let you drive her away— not from this place, not from my life.*

My chest burned. After so much silence, his words ignited a fire inside me. He was saying it. At last, he was saying it before everyone.

But Emilio was not a man to surrender. He loomed over his son, his presence like a wall.

—*You fool,* he thundered. *You're letting yourself be dragged into a cheap illusion, by a girl who has nothing to offer you.*

The ground crumbled beneath me. His words cut deep— though they no longer surprised me. I closed my eyes a moment, searching for strength in the heavens.

When I opened them again, I saw Ron step forward. His voice shook with emotion, but it was unbreakable.

—*She offers me everything. She gives me what you cannot understand, Father: faith, tenderness, honesty. She is the person God placed in my path, and nothing you say will change that.*

88

The murmur rose again, louder this time, like a river breaking its banks. Faces revealed shock, disapproval… but others, quiet smiles of sympathy.

The pastor tried to intervene.

—*Please, brothers, let us remain calm…*

But Emilio silenced him with a single, harsh gesture. His eyes never left Ron.

—*Is this how you repay me? Is this how you dishonor your family, your name?*

Ron drew in a deep breath, and in that moment I saw him—saw him transform before my eyes. He was no longer the boy who bowed his head before his father. He was a man.

—*It is not dishonor, Father. It is love.*

The sanctuary erupted again in whispers and gasps. My tears flowed freely now, but they were not tears of fear. They were pride—blazing, unstoppable pride.

Emilio gritted his teeth, his voice a roar.

—*I forbid you to see her! I forbid you to speak to her, to think of her, even to dream of her!*

Ron turned to me then. His eyes met mine, fierce and steady. In them I saw something unbreakable.

—*You cannot forbid it anymore.*

Time froze. Emilio shaking with rage, Ron standing

unyielding, and me—tears streaming, feeling something inside me shatter… not to die, but to be set free.

I rose from my seat. My legs trembled, but I walked forward, step by trembling step. The murmur swelled around me. I stopped beside Ron. And there, before them all, I lifted my voice.

—*I love him too.*

The silence fell like a veil. Not even a breath stirred. Only the pounding of my heart like a drum.

Emilio's eyes widened in fury, as if unable to fathom my defiance.

—*Shut your mouth!* he bellowed.

But my voice would not be silenced.

—*I will not shut up any longer,* I said, trembling but resolute. *I am not ashamed of what I feel. It is not a mistake, not a stain, not a whim. It is love, and I will not deny it.*

The pastor tried once more to calm the storm.

—*Brother Emilio, please, this is not the place…*

But Emilio brushed him aside with a harsh movement. His glare pinned me as if he could crush me with it.

—*You… you don't know what you're saying.*

—*I know exactly what I'm saying,* I answered, my trembling voice growing clearer, stronger. *And I know God does not shame true love.*

The murmur shifted. Some nodded quietly, some clapped with hesitant courage. Doubt lingered on certain faces, but others shone with silent solidarity.

Emilio looked around, and for the first time, I saw him falter. His authority—the unshakable weight he always carried—was cracking in front of dozens of witnesses.

Ron stepped closer to me. He took my hand, his fingers locking tightly with mine. The touch ran through me like fire, steady and absolute.

—*Father,* he said, his voice like a verdict, *you cannot separate what is already united.*

The silence that followed cut like the edge of a blade.

Emilio's breathing grew ragged, his face hardened, his eyes aflame. For a moment I thought he would explode again, scream, strike, unleash all his fury.

But then... his shoulders dropped, just barely, as though the weight of the world had finally crashed down upon him.

—*I will never accept it...* he muttered. But it no longer sounded like a roar. It sounded like a man broken. *I will not accept it. But... I cannot fight it either.*

His words lingered, harsh yet defeated. A surrender, unwilling but undeniable.

Ron gripped my hand tighter. My knees trembled, but my heart filled with a strange, liberating peace. We had won. Not because Emilio had blessed us, not because the whispers of the town would stop. We had won because he finally understood: he could not destroy what we were.

And right there, in that temple thick with murmurs, I knew—the storm had passed.

The gathering ended without hymns, without order. People filed out in clusters, whispering, staring at us with eyes that no longer pierced as sharply.

Ron and I remained at the altar, still hand in hand. The pastor approached with worry in his eyes, but also a tender kindness.

—*Children, I do not know what paths await you,* he said softly. *But if you walk them together, do it with respect, with faith, with patience. Do not stray from the Lord.*

We both nodded. I pressed the letter hidden in my Bible, no longer a secret, but a promise.

Outside, the sunlight struck our faces, like a breath after drowning. The plaza buzzed with neighbors who hadn't entered the church but already knew what had happened. Eyes followed us—some reproachful, some secretly approving.

I didn't care.

Ron laced his fingers through mine, and we walked side by side, in the full light of day, without hiding.

—*At last,* he whispered close to my ear, *at last I can walk with you without fear.*

Tears welled again.

—*We made it.*

He gave me a weary but victorious smile.

—*No… God made it through us.*

That afternoon we sat beneath the shade of a great tree in the plaza. Words felt too small after everything. We simply looked at each other, as if to carve every detail into memory—proof that, despite everything, we had endured.

I rested my head on his shoulder, listening to his heartbeat. I thought of all the nights I had wept alone, convinced I had lost him. The humiliation, the rejection, the endless shadows… And yet here he was. Real. Warm. Unbroken.

—*Do you know what I kept in my Bible?* I asked softly.

—*What?*

—*Your letter.*

Ron smiled, brushing his hand over mine.

—*Then I know it will never be lost.*

The days that followed were strange. Emilio barely spoke to us. He passed us with that hard, distant stare.

Not acceptance, not blessing... but no longer opposition. His silence was its own surrender.

The stares of the town remained, the whispers never fully ceased. But I no longer crumbled beneath them. I had Ron. And every time I saw him smile, I knew the rest was nothing but noise.

One evening, as we walked home, Ron stopped suddenly. He took both my hands, his eyes blazing.

—*Esther,* he said, *I don't know what lies ahead. My father may never change. The people may never stop talking. But know this: I will not let go of your hand.*

Tears blurred my vision.

—*Nor I yours.*

He smiled, leaning closer.

—*Then whatever comes, we've already won.*

And there, in the dusty street, with no shadows to hide us, he kissed me. Not the stolen kiss of the first time, nor the trembling kiss of secrecy. But a firm kiss, an open kiss, a fearless kiss—the kiss of someone who no longer hides.

That night, before sleeping, I opened my Bible and touched the letter between its pages. But I no longer needed to read it for hope. It had become a symbol, a reminder of the darkness we had walked through and left behind.

I knelt as always, but my words were no lament this time.

— *Thank You, Lord,* I whispered, smiling through tears. *Thank You for never letting us go.*

And as I lay down, eyes closing, a certainty filled me: the future was uncertain, yes, but it was in His hands. And in those hands, with Ron by my side, I was safe.

The last thing I remembered before drifting into sleep was the echo of Ron's voice in the church:

"It is love, and I will not deny it."

That phrase would be my anthem. Our banner.

And with it, I knew… the storm was over.

The End

EPILOGUE

The mirror that stared back at me wasn't large or shining. It hung on the wall of my room, an old mirror that had once belonged to my mother, its wooden frame chipped and scarred by time. Yet that morning, when I looked into it, I saw something I had never seen before: a woman about to be married.

My dress wasn't anything from a glossy magazine. It was simple, ivory white, stitched by loving hands in the neighborhood, a gift of labor and affection. The veil barely brushed my shoulders, and my hands trembled as I adjusted it again and again. It wasn't the fabric that made it beautiful, but what it meant. It was proof that we had come this far, that God had heard every tear, every prayer, every silence.

— *You look beautiful,* Aunt Lorena whispered from the doorway, her eyes shining.

I smiled, because the same woman who had once told me I was "risking my future" was now here, straightening a fold of my dress with trembling fingers. Life sometimes takes turns even the wildest dreamer could never imagine.

The church was not draped in costly flowers, nor did golden candelabras glow along the aisles. Only a few paper garlands, made by the children of the congregation, hung from the walls. On the altar, a bouquet of wildflowers, gathered that very morning by Mateo and his family.

When I entered, holding my eldest cousin's arm, my heart pounded so fiercely I thought the floor would echo it back. Each step across the wooden boards whispered memories of all that had happened between these walls. Here was where our eyes first met with that burning intensity. Here was where Emilio had humiliated us before everyone. And here—today—we would seal our love with God's blessing.

The murmurs faded. Everyone stood. And at the front, waiting by the altar, was Ron.

His suit was dark and plain, borrowed from a friend. But in his eyes blazed a light that pierced through me. It wasn't the clothes that made him shine—it was the barely contained smile, the tremor in his hands, the certainty that he had waited for this moment as long as I had.

98

The pastor spoke simple words, yet each fell like balm upon my heart. He spoke of love that endures, love that refuses to surrender, love that stands even in the storm.

I barely heard half of it. My gaze kept returning to Ron. In his eyes I saw every secret meeting, every hushed whisper, the letter still tucked inside my Bible, the stolen kisses beneath the shade of a tree. And now, before the entire congregation, we no longer had to hide.

When the moment came for our vows, my voice trembled.

—*I promise to walk with you, even when the road grows dark. I promise to hold your hand when you feel you cannot go on. I promise to pray with you, to laugh with you, to weep with you. I promise never to let go of what God Himself placed in our hearts.*

A murmur swept the church. Some wept openly. Others smiled.

Ron looked at me as if I were the only real thing in the entire universe.

—*I promise to honor you, Esther, in abundance and in want. I promise to defend your name, even if the whole world tries to stain it. I promise your smile will be my triumph, and your tears my battle. And before God, I promise never to leave your side.*

My legs nearly gave way. The pastor asked us to join

hands and prayed over us. And when he said, *"You may kiss the bride,"* the entire church burst into applause.

The kiss was not long, not burning with passion. It was tender, sweet, just enough to seal the promise. It was the kiss of two souls who had waited too long and could finally breathe.

Tears blurred my vision. It all felt like a dream. Children laughed, hands clapped with joy, and music rose—simple guitars, cheerful palms.

And then I saw him.

At the very back, standing, was Emilio.

He had not entered with the rest, nor had he sat close. He stood alone, firm, his face stern. His impeccable suit made him look all the more imposing. For a few tense seconds, I feared he would break it all again with one harsh word.

But he didn't.

When our eyes met, Emilio did not speak. Slowly, he lowered his head—like a man conceding defeat, or perhaps like someone finally understanding what he had resisted for far too long.

And though he did not smile, that gesture was enough.

My heart clenched. Because in that silence, he gave me the greatest reconciliation he could ever offer.

The celebration was no lavish banquet. It was held in the

churchyard, with long tables covered in borrowed, colorful cloths. The food was simple, prepared by the sisters of the congregation—rice, stewed chicken, freshly baked bread. Yet to me, everything tasted of a heavenly feast.

Music filled the air, children ran between tables, and laughter rang out. Ron and I could not stop looking at each other, smiling like two teenagers who still couldn't believe what had just happened.

Mateo came to me and wrapped me in a tight embrace.

—*I told you, Esther... nothing that is true can ever be destroyed.*

—*Thank you for being our messenger,* I said, remembering the letter.

He chuckled, winking playfully.

—*I always knew you two were meant to be.*

Later in the afternoon, I saw Emilio standing alone near one of the tables, quietly observing everything. Summoning my courage, I walked toward him. My hands still trembled, but I couldn't let the day pass without speaking to him.

I stopped in front of him.

—*Thank you for coming.*

Emilio's eyes were hard, but no anger burned there. Instead, I saw the weariness of a man who had fought too long against the current.

—I didn't come willingly, he admitted at last, his voice low and grave. *I came because... I needed to see with my own eyes that it was true.*

I swallowed hard but held my ground.

—And now that you've seen... what do you think?

A long silence. Then Emilio lowered his gaze.

—I think... that what endures for so long cannot be an illusion.

He said nothing more. He didn't embrace me, didn't bless me. But those words cracked the armor he had carried for years. And for me, that was the greatest gift he could have given.

As the sun dipped low, painting the church walls in shades of gold, Ron and I slipped away from the bustle. Hand in hand, we walked to the old tree that had once sheltered our trembling first kiss.

I leaned against his chest, feeling the world finally settle in our favor.

—Do you remember this place? he asked, brushing his fingers through my hair.

—Of course, I smiled. *This is where it all began.*

Ron's lips curved into a quiet smile.

—And this is where it begins again.

We kissed—this time with no fear of being discovered,

no dread of an angry voice interrupting us. It was a kiss free of shadows, clean and unburdened, with the whole future open before us.

That night, when the last guest had left and the church stood empty, I knelt at the very altar where I had shed so many tears. But these tears were different.

—*Thank You, Lord,* I whispered. *Thank You for never letting go of me. Thank You for showing me that Your love is stronger than every whisper, every rejection, every obstacle.*

Ron knelt beside me, taking my hand.

—*This is only the beginning,* he murmured.

I looked at him—and knew he was right.

Life would not be easy. I knew it. Emilio would remain a man of stern character. The neighborhood would keep talking. Poverty would still weigh on my home and my days.

But I no longer cared. Because I no longer walked alone.

The love we had defended with tears and unyielding faith was now our shield. And though the future held trials, we would face them together.

With faith.

With hope.

With love.

That night I fell asleep with a truth carved into my soul: every struggle had been worth it.

Because in the end, love had not only bound Ron and me together. It had broken chains, torn down walls, and lit a flame in the darkness.

And that flame—I knew with all my heart—would never be extinguished.

The End.

ACKNOWLEDGMENTS

First, to God—the Author of life and of every story. To Him, who in the midst of the deepest silence taught me that there is always a whisper of love stronger than any rumor, and that even in the hardest trial, hope blooms. Without His guidance, His comfort, and His infinite patience, these pages would never have seen the light.

To my family, for being solid ground in the middle of the storm, for teaching me through their example that faith is not a theory but a path walked daily with love, sacrifice, and trust. Their words, their gestures, and even their silences inspired me to shape my characters and breathe real life into these pages.

To my friends, who with affection, counsel, and even hard questions helped me see this story from different angles. You reminded me that stories born from the heart have the power to touch other hearts as well.

To every reader holding this book in their hands: thank you. Thank you for opening not only your eyes but also your soul to this Christian love story that seeks to be more than entertainment—that longs to be a companion in nights of doubt, a ray of light in dark days, a reflection that true love and authentic faith still exist. You are the reason words become bridges, encounters, and silent miracles.

To those who have loved in secret, to those who have faced opposition, to those who have felt the world pressing against their dreams: this book is yours too. For I know you will understand every sigh, every tear, and every smile Esther and Ron share within these pages.

Finally, to all who believe in second chances, in forgiveness, and in the power of love that is born in God—my gratitude is eternal. Because it is you who keep alive the certainty that even in a world full of noise and silence, there will always be one voice that resounds louder: the voice of true love.

Nuriss Clark

Is a woman whose life embodies resilience, purpose, and transformation.

She graduated in Theology from LOGOS Christian University in Jacksonville, Florida, holding an Associate Degree in Biblical Studies. She is also a licensed Real Estate Broker in both Florida and New York.

In her twenties, she opened her first real estate office in Brooklyn, NY, and thanks to high sales volume, she was recognized by Dunn & Bradstreet as a new company generating millions in sales during its first quarter.

For over 20 years, she has worked in various areas of real estate—residential, commercial, and industrial. She has also served as a mortgage broker, insurance agent, tax and accounting specialist, with extensive knowledge of FHA, VA, conventional loans, and other financial products.

Her story is a living testimony to the power of faith, perseverance, and God's grace.

From nothing, she became a businesswoman, investor, and now a motivational author, committed to inspiring others to never give up.

www.ingramcontent.com/pod-product-compliance
Lightning Source LLC
Chambersburg PA
CBHW070500130626

46555CB00003B/1093